# WE CAN READ!™

# Pond Monster

*by* Jacqueline Sweeney

*photography by* G. K. & Vikki Hart
*photo illustration by* Blind Mice Studio

**BENCHMARK BOOKS**

MARSHALL CAVENDISH
NEW YORK

*For Hoyte, whose discerning heart
embraces the spectrum but sends
the monsters away.*

*With thanks to Daria Murphy, reading specialist and
principal of Scotchtown Elementary, Goshen, New York,
for reading this manuscript with care and for writing the
"We Can Read and Learn" activity guide.*

Benchmark Books
Marshall Cavendish
99 White Plains Road
Tarrytown, New York 10591-9001
Website:www.marshallcavendish.com

Text copyright © 2002 by Jacqueline Sweeney
Photo illustrations © 2002 by G.K. & Vikki Hart
and Mark and Kendra Empey

Library of Congress Cataloging-in-Publication Data
Sweeney, Jacqueline.
Pond Monster / by Jacqueline Sweeney.
p. cm. — (We can read!)
Summary: Animal friends discover that the horrible monster
in the pond is really a rainbow trout.
ISBN 0-7614-1123-2
[1. Trout—Fiction. 2. Animals—Fiction. 3. Monsters—Fiction.] I. Title.
PZ7.S974255 Po 2001          [E]—dc21          00-066734

Printed in Italy

1 3 5 6 4 2

# Characters

Molly

Eddie

Hildy

Jim (J. P.)

Tim

The Owls

Ron

Gus

Ladybug

$M$olly and Eddie
were sitting on Pond Rock.

*SPLASH!*

"What was that?" asked Molly.

"I can't tell," said Eddie.

"It's too far away."

Molly and Eddie stared into the pond.

They saw a flash of silver,
a flash of green.

*Quack! Quack!*

Flap! Flap!

"Monster!" yelled Hildy.

"It has black spots!

It came right at me!"

"Are you sure?" asked Eddie.

"I'm sure," said Hildy.

"It has a red stripe.

It's six feet long.

We should warn the others."

$E$ddie ran to Bunny Hollow.

"Pond Monster!" he shouted.

"It has sharp claws.

It's slimy and green."

J. P. and Tim ran to Owl Woods.

"Pond Monster!" they shouted.

"It has silver eyes.

It's scary and mean."

The Owls told Ron.

Ron told Gus,

"It's as tall as the sky.

It growls and spits fire!"

Ladybug flew by.

"It has hot red eyes."

"It eats bugs!" she huffed.

17

"I'm afraid to sleep," said Tim.

Ron croaked, "I'm afraid to swim."

So the friends decided to watch the pond.

Ron and Hildy watched from Pond Rock.

Gus watched from the reeds.

Eddie watched from a tall tree.

Jim and Tim hid inside a log.

But Molly was bravest of all.
She watched from a tiny branch.

*SPLASH!*

"Pond Monster!" cried Hildy.

"Pond Monster!" cried Ron.

"It's right under Molly!"

Molly was shaking.

Her branch was shaking too.

Suddenly it snapped.

"Help!" she cried.

*Splish!*

She fell in!

There was a flash of silver,
a flash of green.
Something swam under Molly
and pushed her to shore.

A fish leaped in the air.
Its colors gleamed.

"It has a red stripe!" said Hildy.

"Like a rainbow," whispered Ron.

"What is it?" asked Molly.

"I know," said Ladybug.

"It's not a monster."

"It's a *rainbow trout*."

# WE CAN READ AND LEARN

The following activities are designed to enhance literacy development. *Pond Monster* can help children build skills in vocabulary, phonics, and creative writing; explore self-awareness; and make connections between literature and other subject areas such as science and math.

## MONSTER CHALLENGE WORDS

There are many challenging vocabulary words in this story. Children can draw curved lines in the shape of a rainbow. (Remember, there's a rainbow trout in the story!) After discussing the meaning of each of the words, children can put them in alphabetical order from the top of the rainbow to the bottom. This list can help you to get started.

| | | | |
|---|---|---|---|
| air | branch | brave | claws |
| eyes | flash | gleam | green |
| growl | mean | monster | scary |
| shake | sharp | shore | silver |
| slimy | snap | spit | spots |
| stripe | trout | warn | watch |

## FUN WITH PHONICS RAINBOW

Draw a rainbow with five sections. Draw a line down the center, dividing the rainbow in half. Label one side of the rainbow, "short vowel words," the other, "long vowel words." Label each line of the rainbow with a vowel (a, e, i, o, u). Help children find words from the story that have the same vowel sound and place them on the correct side (short vowel or long vowel) of the rainbow.

**Here are some words to get started:**

Short "a" words:    at, black, snap, and, swam
Long "a" words:    came, day, rain, shake, brave
Short "e" words:    tell, red, fell, next
Long "e" words:    me, green, mean, leap
Short "i" words:    six, spit, it, Jim, Tim
Long "i" words:    right, stripe, fire, by
Short "o" words:    pond, rock, spot, Molly
Long "o" words:    told, hollow, rainbow
Short "u" words:    but, Gus, bunny, under
Long "u" words    you, too (Not all these words have the letter "u," but they do have the sounds of a long "u" word, as in tune.)

## THE BLACK-SPOTTED, RED-STRIPED, SIX-FOOT-LONG, SHARP-CLAWED, SLIMY, GREEN, SILVER-EYED POND MONSTER!

In the story, Hildy thought she saw a monster that was six feet long with black spots and a red stripe. Eddie told the others that it had sharp claws and was slimy and green. By the end of the story the description has changed, and everyone is frightened. Help children to develop speaking and listening skills with an old-fashioned game of telephone. Start out with a simple sentence such as, "It has black spots, and it is six feet long." Each child (or adult) can whisper the sentence to a neighbor and pass it on. At the end of the line, find out what the original sentence turned into. This is a great way to discuss the importance of good communication skills.

31

## About the author

Jacqueline Sweeney is a poet and children's author. She has worked with children and teachers for over twenty-five years implementing writing workshops in schools throughout the United States. She specializes in motivating reluctant writers and shares her creative teaching methods in numerous professional books for teachers. She lives in Stone Ridge, New York.

## About the photo illustrations

The photo illustrations are the collaborative effort of photographers G. K. and Vikki Hart and Blind Mice Studio. Following Mark Empey's sketched storyboard, G. K. and Vikki Hart photograph each animal and element individually. The images are then scanned and manipulated, pixel by pixel, by Mark and Kendra Empey at Blind Mice Studio.

Each charming illustration may contain from 15 to 30 individual photographs.

All the animals that appear in this book were handled with love. They have been returned to or adopted by loving homes.